Christopher Churchmouse Classics®

A SHORT TAIL

"Man looks at the outward appearance, but the Lord looks at the heart"
—1 Samuel 16:7 (NIV).

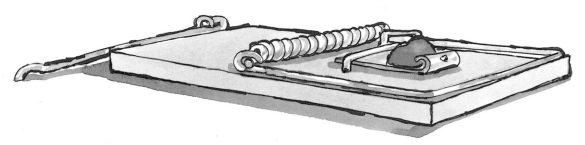

WRITTEN BY BARBARA DAVOLL
Pictures by Dennis Hockerman

A Sonflower Book

VICTOR BOOKS®

A DIVISION OF SCRIPTURE PRESS PUBLICATIONS INC.
USA CANADA ENGLAND

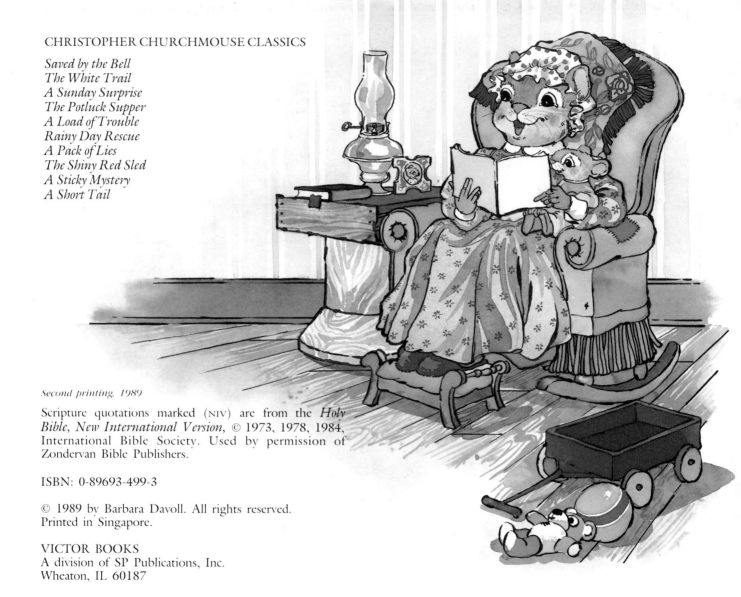

CHRISTOPHER CHURCHMOUSE CLASSICS

Second printing, 1989

Scripture quotations marked (NIV) are from the *Holy Bible, New International Version*, © 1973, 1978, 1984, International Bible Society. Used by permission of Zondervan Bible Publishers.

ISBN: 0-89693-499-3

VICTOR BOOKS
A division of SP Publications, Inc.
Wheaton, IL 60187

A Word to Parents and Teachers

The Christopher Churchmouse Classics will please both the eyes and ears of children, and help them grow in the knowledge of God.

This book, *A Short Tail,* one of the character-building stories in the series, is about appearance.

"Man looks at the outward appearance,
but the Lord looks at the heart"
—1 Samuel 16:7 (NIV).

Through this story about Christopher, children will see a practical application of this Bible truth.

Use the Discussion Starters on page 24 to help children remember the story and the valuable lesson it teaches. Happy reading!

Christopher's Friend,

Barbara Davall

hristopher Churchmouse came to an abrupt stop in the middle of the church hall. What was that awful sound he was hearing? He perked up his ears to hear better. The cries were coming from the church kitchen.

Running to the kitchen, he saw the reason for the noise. Underneath the sink was a huge trap. Caught right inside the trap was his smallest cousin, Ned. Christopher knew that Ned would not be alive for long if he did not help him. There was no time to call his papa or grandpa.

I'll just have to spring that trap with my paw, he thought to himself. Christopher knew it was very dangerous for him to do this. He knew he could

4

very easily get his own paw stuck in
the trap, but seeing his little cousin in
such pain made him ignore the
danger.

He's so little, thought Christopher.
I've got to help him.

5

"It's OK, Ned," he said in a soothing voice. "I'll get you out of there."

"Oh, hurry, Christopher—please hurry!" cried the sad little mouse.

Christopher put his paw close to the part of the trap that was holding Ned's foot.

"Now, Ned, listen. Listen very carefully," said Christopher. "I'm going to put my paw right here and lift the spring. When I do, you pull your foot out. Understand?"

"Uh-huh," gulped Ned.

"All right. Are you ready? Here we go. One—two—three!" and

6

Christopher thrust his own little paw into the trap, lifting it just enough so that Ned could get free. Then Christopher quickly pulled his own paw out and turned to run. SNAP! The trap slammed down on his tail.

"Ouch!" yelped Christopher.

Ned was lying in a curled-up ball, whimpering and licking his wounds.

He didn't even notice that Christopher's tail was caught in the trap. Christopher looked around wildly wondering how he could free himself. Then he thought that because his tail was so skinny he could get it out if he pulled hard enough. He grabbed his tail and jerked it quickly. It came out of the trap!

"Ouch!" said Christopher, trying
to turn around and look at his tail.
"That really hurt!" But he didn't
have too much time to think about it
because Ned needed help quickly.
Christopher was sure that Ned's foot
was broken. Somehow Chris would
have to get him back to his home.

"Ned, can you hang on if I
put you up on my back?"

"I'll try," sobbed the little
mouse.

"Let's try not to hurt your
foot. Just grab hold
of my fur."

Ned grabbed Christopher's
fur and pulled himself up
onto Chris' back.

Chris wasn't a very big mouse himself, so the trip back to Ned's home was long and hard. When Chris got to the door, he shoved it with his foot, and they both tumbled into the living room. Christopher's Aunt Snootie was sitting on the sofa with her sewing basket.

"Why—what on earth? Oh, my Neddy, what has happened to you?" Aunt Snootie rushed over to her little mouse. "Oh, my poor little dear," she said, picking him up and carrying him to bed.

9

Christopher knew Ned was in good hands. He slipped out the door quietly and ran for his own home and his own mama.

He rushed in the door and gasped, "O Mama, a terrible thing happened! Ned was caught in a trap!"

"Oh no!" exclaimed Mama. "That's the worst possible thing that can happen to a mouse."

"He's all right though, Mama," said Christopher quickly, not wishing to worry her. "He's all right because I freed him and carried him home. I think his foot is broken, though."

"O Son, you've had a hard time," said Mama, going over to give him a hug. "Christopher!" she exclaimed, stepping back. "Your tail!"

"Wh—what's wrong with my tail, Mama?"

"Christopher, you must have caught it in the trap. You've lost part of your tail."

"I have?" said Christopher, trying to turn around to see his tail.

"Well, you didn't cut it all off," said Mama. "Just a little. Let's go into the kitchen, and I'll fix it up for you."

Soon Mama had his tail all cleaned up and bandaged.

11

By evening Christopher didn't feel
very well at all. In fact, he was just
plain sick. Mama put him in bed,
gave him some hot soup, and talked
soothingly to him. Soon he fell asleep.
    For the next few days Christopher
didn't feel like doing much. Every
    morning Mama would come
      in and fluff up his pillows,
      give him extra special good
        things to eat, and tell him
        how Ned was doing.
        Sometimes she would

read funny books to him, but most of the time Christopher just lay in bed and rested.

One day Mama said, "Christopher, I think you can get up today. We'll take the bandage off."

Christopher said, "Oh good! Can I watch in the mirror while you do it?"

"Sure," said Mama as she began to unwind the bandage.

Christopher kept twisting his neck backward to see in the mirror. "Mama, I'm sure glad you know how to fix my tail. It will be long again, won't it?"

"I hope so," Mama said as she unwound the bandage carefully.

"Mama, can't you unwind the bandage faster? I can't wait to see my tail."

Every time Christopher twisted his neck to look in the mirror, he moved his tail a little. Mama finally said, "Christopher Churchmouse, please stand still!"

"Sorry, Mama, I just can't wait to see my tail."

Finally Mama had the bandage unwound.

"Mama, it looks just like it did when I cut it off!" Christopher said in a disappointed whisper.

"Yes, Christopher." Mama shook her head sadly.

"Mama, it looks so funny! What will I do with a short tail? Everybody will make fun of me."

"Now, Christopher, I'm sure they won't."

"Oh yes they will, Mama! I *know* they will! They'll all stand around and laugh at me."

"Your friends won't be that way. Let's not worry about it anymore. You don't need a long tail anyway. Come on, let's go take a walk."

"Mama," said Christopher, "I'm not feeling very well right now."

"You aren't?" asked Mama anxiously.

"No, I think I'll just stay at home and rest some more."

"All right," said Mama, and she went for a walk alone. She knew that Christopher did not want to go out because he thought people would make fun of his tail.

15

That evening when Papa Churchmouse came home from work, Mama said, "Papa, we have a problem. Christopher does not want to go out because of his tail. He thinks his friends will make fun of him. What are we going to do?"

"I'll talk to him," said Papa.

Later that evening as Christopher was getting ready for bed, Papa came into his room.

"How are you feeling tonight, Son?" asked Papa.

"Oh, all right," said Christopher.

"Good!" said Papa. "Then you can go to school tomorrow."

"But I may not feel so good tomorrow."

"You're worried about your tail, aren't you?" said Papa kindly, sitting down on Christopher's bed.

"Well—yes—I . . ."

"Christopher, do you remember the Bible verse the teacher taught the class last Sunday?" asked Papa. Christopher and his family lived in the church, so they always went to Sunday School with the boys and girls.

"Sure," said Christopher. " 'Man looks at the outward appearance, but the Lord looks at the heart.' "

"Do you know what that verse means?" asked Papa.

"I think so," said Christopher.

"The teacher said others see only the outside of us, which is just our house. Our real self lives inside our body."

"Do you also remember the teacher saying the Lord looks inside at the real you?" asked Papa.

"Yes," said Chris.

"Since the Lord looks on the inside of us, which do you think we should think about more—the outside or the inside?" continued Papa.

"Well—the inside, I guess," said Christopher thoughtfully.

"I think so too," said Papa, stooping to kiss him good night. "If that's true, then a shorter tail doesn't seem to matter so much, does it?" said Papa.

"I see what you mean," murmured the sleepy little mouse.

"Thank you, Papa."

The next morning Christopher awoke early. He pulled on his stubby tail, trying to make it as long as he could. With a sigh he took a look in the mirror and knew there was just no way to make it look like a regular tail. Squaring his shoulders, he looked at himself in the mirror and said, "That's all right. What counts is what's on the inside, and I'm not going to worry about the outside anymore."

At breakfast he surprised Mama by saying, "I'm not even going to care when the other mice make fun of me. I know they're going to tease me because of my tail, but it really doesn't matter what I look like. That's what Papa said last night, and that's right, isn't it, Mama?"

"That's right, Son," said Mama, proudly looking at her little mouse.

When he got to school, he noticed that his friends were all in a corner over in one part of the room.

Some of them were looking at him. Taking a deep breath, he walked over to the group of mice. "Hi, everyone."

"Welcome back, Christopher!" said one mouse.

"We heard all about you saving Ned's life," said another.

21

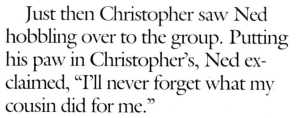

Just then Christopher saw Ned hobbling over to the group. Putting his paw in Christopher's, Ned exclaimed, "I'll never forget what my cousin did for me."

Christopher's teacher walked over to the group, smiling. She put her paw around Christopher's shoulders and said, "We're delighted to have such a brave hero in our class, aren't we?" At that the mice children began to clap and cheer.

Christopher thought he would burst with happiness. *I can't wait to tell Papa,* he thought. *He was right. We've all learned that what's on the inside is more important than what's on the outside. My silly, short tail really doesn't matter after all.*

DISCUSSION STARTERS

1. Where was the trap located, and who was caught in it?
2. What dangerous thing did Christopher do to rescue Ned?
3. What happened to Christopher as he was rescuing Ned?
4. Why didn't Christopher want to go to school after his accident?
5. Did the mice children laugh at Christopher the way he thought they would?
6. What does the Lord see when He looks at us—the inside or the outside?

    What do we usually see when we look at others?

    Ask the Lord to help you look on the inside as He does.